TO Tenisha Diane Brown

DISNEY'S
SMALL WORLD LIBRARY
DONALD AND THE TROLL
An Adventure in Norway

GROLIER ENTERPRISES INC.
DANBURY, CONNECTICUT

© 1991 The Walt Disney Company. All rights reserved.
Printed in the United States of America.
Developed by the Walt Disney Company in conjunction with Nancy Hall, Inc.
ISBN: 0-7172-8229-5

Donald and his nephews were spending their summer vacation in Norway. They were on their way to board a cruise ship when Donald stumbled on a strange-looking rock. Dewey picked it up.

"This rock is shaped just like a troll," he said, handing it to Donald. "I read a Norwegian fairy tale about trolls once. It said that trolls are legendary creatures who supposedly come out at night to make trouble for people. Then they have to scurry back to their caves before the light of day, otherwise the sun will turn them into stones."

"Hey, Uncle Donald" said Louie, laughing. "Maybe that stone you're holding was a slow troll who didn't make it back to his cave on time!"

But Donald wasn't laughing. He dropped the stone immediately!

After they had boarded the ship, Huey noticed a painting of a magnificent ship.

"That's a Viking ship," he said. "The Vikings were brave explorers who lived in and around Norway long ago."

"Yes, and they sailed in these very waters," added Donald.

"I bet the Vikings didn't sail in ships like this one!" said Louie, peering into the main dining hall. "This boat is more like a floating hotel!"

"Your table is right this way," said the friendly steward.

"Let's eat!" said Huey happily.

After lunch Donald and the boys went up on deck to admire the beautiful scenery. Then suddenly the walls of the cliffs seemed to close in on them.

"This river is getting awfully narrow here," said Dewey.

"This is a fjord," explained Donald. "Icy glaciers carved these waterways deep into the mountains a long time ago."

Before long the fjord widened again.

"Wow!" said Louie. "Fjords are neat! Look at those caves up there in the cliffs!"

"I wonder if there are any trolls living in there," said Donald, shivering.

At that moment a big gust of wind blew Donald's cap off his head. Before it hit the deck, a puppy came scrambling from out of nowhere and caught it in her teeth.

"Hey, come back here with that!" called Donald, and the chase was on!

"Oh, no!" he cried as the puppy tripped a waiter who was carrying a tray loaded with desserts.

Before the mischievous puppy could run off, Huey
dived and grabbed her.

"Nice save!" boomed the voice of the captain, taking
the puppy from Huey. "I promised my son a puppy for his
birthday, but I can't seem to keep this one out of trouble!"

"No kidding!" muttered Donald.

Later Donald and the boys had dinner. They walked around the deck for a while and soon it was time for bed.

"Which do you think are scarier?" asked Dewey, as he climbed into the top bunk. "Giants or trolls?"

"That's easy," answered Huey. "Giants—because they're so big."

"No, trolls," said Louie. "They're small and they can hide almost anywhere—even under beds!"

Before long, the boys were making up troll stories,
each more scary than the one before.

"That's enough for now," said Donald. "It's time we all
tried to get some sleep!"

But Donald was too scared to sleep. Try as he might,
he just couldn't stop thinking about the trolls. He tossed
and turned until it was morning.

That morning the ship docked in a town called Stavanger.

"We'll be stopping here overnight," announced the steward. "Enjoy your day of sightseeing."

"If I can stay awake," grumbled Donald, rubbing his eyes.

As they were walking down the gangplank, they saw the captain.

"How is the puppy doing?" Dewey asked.

"She got away again," answered the captain sadly.
"But this time I don't think I'll find her. One of the
passengers saw her run off the ship. My little boy is going
to be so disappointed."

"We'll look for her," said Huey.

"Sure, I'll bet we can find her," agreed Dewey.

Donald and the boys went into the part of town called Old Stavanger. As they walked down the cobblestone streets, the boys looked around for the puppy. They peeked into alleyways that separated the charming old buildings. They looked under benches and even under parked cars. But they didn't see her anywhere.

"Excuse me," said a boy. "My name is Per Jorgensen. Are you looking for something?"

"We're looking for a puppy," said Dewey. "She belongs to the captain of our ship. She ran off the boat when we docked."

Per thought for a moment. "Maybe the puppy has returned to the harbor to find the ship," he said. "Let's ask some of the fishermen if anyone there has seen her."

They all walked back to the harbor. When they got to the docks, Per went from boat to boat asking each fisherman if he had seen the puppy. But no one had.

"Well, we tried our best," said Louie. "Maybe the captain had better luck."

They kept walking until they came to their cruise ship.

"What a beautiful ship!" said Per. "I've always wanted to go on a big ship like that! Do you have your own rooms? Have you seen the engines?"

"Maybe you can come aboard and we can give you a tour tomorrow before we set sail," said Dewey. "I'm sure the captain won't mind."

"Do you really think so?" asked Per, hopefully. "That would be wonderful!"

Per looked at his watch. "It's time for me to meet my mother back in town," he said.

"We'll walk you back," said Donald. "I'd like to see more of the town, anyway."

When they arrived back in Old Stavanger, Per ran over to greet his mother.

"Mother, I'd like you to meet my new friends," said Per. "This is their first trip to Norway."

"Welcome," said Mrs. Jorgensen as they all introduced themselves. "Would you like to join us for lunch? We don't live far from here."

"That's the best idea I've heard all day!" said Donald.

In a little while they arrived at Per's house at the edge
of town. While Mrs. Jorgensen prepared their lunch, Per
took his guests for a walk in some nearby woods.

Although it was a sunny day, the woods were dark and
mysterious. Donald's imagination began to run away with
him.

"Do you believe in trolls?" he asked Per.

Per laughed. "No, but many people believe that these woods are filled with them," he replied.

Donald began to get very nervous. The woods looked like a good hiding place for a troll. "Maybe we should head back to the house now," he said.

When they got back to the house, Per's mother served them creamed codfish with boiled potatoes and dill. Everyone agreed the meal was delicious.

After lunch, Donald followed Per into the living room. "What's that?" he asked, pointing to a piece of furniture in the corner.

"It's a loom," said Per. "My mother weaves yarn into rugs. The winters here are very long, and that's what she does to pass the time."

"And my father is a wood carver," Per continued, pointing to a shelf where some scary-looking trolls were standing.

"I don't think Uncle Donald likes trolls very much," said Dewey with a chuckle.

"Don't worry," said Per, noticing the look on Donald's face. "They're only made of wood. We keep them to scare the real ones away," he said, joking.

"I don't think trolls are a laughing matter," Donald muttered.

Then Mrs. Jorgensen called out to the group. "I need some berries for the pie I'm making," she told them. "Would you all go outside and pick some for me?"

"No problem!" said Per, smacking his lips. Then they all raced off into the woods. But Donald was very tired. After missing a whole night's sleep, he was lagging far behind the others.

"Maybe I'll just sit right down here and have a rest," he said to himself. So down he sank into a soft pile of leaves. In no time he was fast asleep, dreaming of trolls.

Donald woke up suddenly when he felt something
cold and damp nudging his cheek.

"Get back, you troll!" he shouted.

When he heard a whimper, he sat up and rubbed his
eyes.

"Hey, you're not a troll!" Donald cried. "You're the captain's puppy! What are you doing here?"

Just then Per and the nephews showed up.

"Uncle Donald!" said Huey. "You found the puppy!"

"I guess I did," said Donald, who wasn't feeling frightened anymore.

"Let's bring her back to the ship right away," said Dewey. "The captain must be worried."

After running back to the house to tell Per's mother the news, they all headed over to the harbor.

When they got back to the dock, the captain and his son were standing on the pier.

"Is this puppy for me?" the little boy cried, as Donald placed her in the boy's arms.

"It sure is!" beamed the captain. "But where on earth did you find her?" he whispered to Donald.

"Let's just say a troll helped me," Donald replied with a grin. "But we couldn't have done it without the help of our new friend, Per."

"I'd like to do something special for you," the captain
told Per after he had heard their tale. "How would you
like to join us for the rest of the cruise? We will be
stopping back in Stavanger in a few days."

Per looked at his mother.

"Go ahead!" she said, smiling.

Per couldn't believe his ears. "Oh, boy!" he cried.
Then he happily ran off with Huey, Dewey, and Louie to
explore the ship.

Did You Know…?

There are many different customs and places that make each country special. Do you remember some of the things below from the story?

Oslo, the capital of Norway, has many outdoor museums. One of the most famous is the museum of Viking ships where visitors can board the same ships the Norwegian explorers used centuries ago.

Norwegians love the outdoors. Skiing, ice skating, hiking, and camping are among the most popular sports. Almost every Norwegian town has its own ski jump and ice rink.

Trolls are creatures from Norwegian folklore.
It is said that trolls often perform tricks on
humans, but legend also has it that they are not
very clever and often end up being tricked in
turn by their victims.

Before Norwegian families open their
presents at Christmastime, they join hands
and walk around the Christmas tree singing
carols. Farm children leave a bowl of
porridge in the barn for an elf who
supposedly watches over the farm animals
on Christmas Eve.

Most Norwegian families eat four meals a
day, and farm families eat as many as
five meals! Favorite foods include
goat cheese, smoked salmon, and
lutefisk (LOOT-fisk), a mushy,
salty codfish. Dig in,
Donald!

Most Norwegians live close to the sea, which they
call the "blue meadow." Many of them are skilled
sailors and are proud of their boats.
The large Norwegian cruise
ships are among the
finest in the world.

Fjords (FEE-ords) are long, narrow, rocky inlets that are found along Norway's coast. The fjords were created by rivers of ice called glaciers millions of years ago. Many of them are breathtakingly beautiful with towering waterfalls, steep rock walls, and dense forests.

During the long winter months, both young and old Norwegians pass the time indoors doing arts and crafts. Jewelrymakers fashion everything from bracelets to silver buttons. Another famous Norwegian craft is *rose maaling* (MAL-ing), in which painters decorate dishes, furniture, and even walls with swirling flowers.